They who can give up essential liberty
to obtain a little temporary safety deserve
neither liberty nor safety.

— BENJAMIN FRANKLIN

THE HOMELAND

DIRECTIVE

The Homeland Directive
© & ™ 2011 Robert Venditti.
Published by Top Shelf Productions
PO Box 1282
Marietta, GA 30061-1282, USA.

Publishers: Chris Staros
and Brett Warnock.
Top Shelf Productions® and the
Top Shelf logo are registered
trademarks of Top Shelf Productions,
Inc. All Rights Reserved. No part of
this publication may be reproduced
without permission, except for small
excerpts for purposes of review.

First Printing, May 2011.
Printed in China.

Visit our online catalog at
www.topshelfcomix.com.

ISBN 978-1-60309-024-7
1. Graphic Novels
2. Political Thriller

CREATED & WRITTEN BY
ROBERT VENDITTI

ILLUSTRATED & COLORED BY
MIKE HUDDLESTON

LETTERING BY
SEAN KONOT

EDITED BY
CHRIS STAROS

BOOK DESIGN BY
JIM TITUS

ONE
THE ROOT
OF ALL EVIL

"OUR ASSESSMENT IS THAT THIS SLIGHT INCREASE IN CHATTER DOES NOT REPRESENT AN IMMEDIATE CONCERN, MR. PRESIDENT.

"C.I.A. HAS ASSURED ME THAT *HUMINT* IS REPORTING NO SPECIFIC TARGETS OR TIMEFRAMES, SO IT COULD BE A RANDOM ANOMALY."

I RECOMMEND THAT WE MAINTAIN AN ELEVATED THREAT CONDITION, AND I WILL, OF COURSE, APPRISE YOU OF ANY SIGNIFICANT DEVELOPMENTS.

THANK YOU, ALBERT.

I HAVE A LUNCH APPOINTMENT WITH THE JAPANESE AMBASSADOR, BUT ANDERS WILL STAY AND HAVE A WORD WITH YOU.

UNTIL OUR NEXT BRIEFING THEN, MR. PRESIDENT.

SIT, ALBERT.

THE PRESIDENT CONTINUES TO HAVE RESERVATIONS IN REGARDS TO YOUR HANDLING OF THE DEPARTMENT.

DOES HE...

THE PRESIDENTIAL ELECTION CYCLE IS BUILDING, AND THE LOSSES SUFFERED IN THE MIDTERMS--AS WELL AS TO THE PRESIDENT'S POLL NUMBERS--*MUST* BE RECOUPED.

THAT CAN'T HAPPEN, UNLESS THE PEOPLE BELIEVE THE PRESIDENT IS DOING EVERYTHING HE CAN TO KEEP THEM SAFE.

ATLANTA.

EXIT 2
Camp Cr Pkwy
Atl Airport

YOU KNOW WHAT THEY SAY: "YOU CAN NEVER BE TOO PREPARED."

YOU DON'T HAVE THAT THING MEMORIZED YET?

"THEY?" YOU'RE THE ONLY ONE I KNOW WHO SAYS THAT, LAURA.

THAT WOULD EXPLAIN THE MESS ON YOUR DESK, AND MY ALWAYS HAVING TO REMIND YOU OF YOUR APPOINTMENTS, AND--

DISORGANIZATION IS A SIGN OF GENIUS. HAVEN'T YOU EVER SEEN EINSTEIN'S HAIR?

YEAH, RIGHT. DR. ARI MUSA, *SUPRA-*GENIUS.

IF YOU'RE SUCH A *GENIUS*, THEN WHY DON'T *YOU* TRY GIVING THE SPEECHES FOR A CHANGE?

WHY DO *I* ALWAYS WIND UP GOING TO THESE STUPID SEMINARS?

WE MAKE A GREAT TEAM, DON'T WE?

THE BEST.

THANKS FOR THE LIFT.

WHAT ARE RESEARCH PARTNERS FOR? I'LL PICK YOU UP ON FRIDAY.

THURSDAY. TRY NOT TO BE LATE.

AND, ARI?

I KNOW, YOU DON'T HAVE TO TELL ME. YOU THINK I'M A GENIUS.

YOU EVER STOP AND CONSIDER HOW LUCKY YOU ARE TO SHARE A LAB WITH ME?

ALL THE TIME.

YEAH.

YOU HAVE YOUR AUTHORIZATION. THERE'S NO ROOM FOR MISTAKES.

IS THERE EVER?

ALL SYSTEMS GO.

WHAT ABOUT THE DOC-ETTE?

JUST STAY WITH OUR TARGET. SHE'S ON SOMEONE ELSE'S TO-DO LIST.

CRUNCH!

UGHH!

DIDN'T YOU SEE THE STOP SIGN?

AW, JEEZ. I'M SORRY. I WASN'T PAYING ATTENTION.

HOW BAD'S THE DAMAGE?

THE BUMPER IS PRETTY BANGED UP.

THANK YOU FOR THE KIND INTRODUCTION, DR. REY.

AND THANK YOU TO THE NEW YORK EPIDEMIOLOGICAL SOCIETY FOR INVITING ME TO SPEAK HERE TONIGHT.

WHILE IT IS TRUE THAT THERE HAVE BEEN EXCITING BREAK-THROUGHS IN VIRAL AND BACTERIOLOGICAL STUDY--

--IT IS TRUER STILL THAT THE ENVIRONMENT WE WORK IN, MUCH LIKE THE ORGANISMS WE TIRELESSLY COMBAT, IS AN EVER-CHANGING ONE.

THE WILL OF OUR SINGLE-CELLED ADVERSARIES TO ADAPT, COUPLED WITH A RISING GLOBAL POPULATION THAT IS INCREASINGLY MOBILE, ARE A DANGEROUS COMBINATION.

FOR EVEN AS MEDICAL ADVANCES GIVE US NEW HOPE, THE AGE-OLD PROCESSES OF MOTHER NATURE ARE AIDED BY THE AMBITIONS OF MAN...

Rnng
Rnng
Rnng

Rnng
Rnn~

WHAT IS IT?

ONE OF OUR LOOSE ENDS IS STILL UNTIED.

HOW?

FIND OUT.

IN THE MEANTIME, GET *BOCA* INVOLVED.

SOMEONE ELSE WAS WAITING. WE DON'T KNOW WHO.

DR. REGAN?

SORRY ABOUT THE CHLOROFORM, BUT WE DIDN'T HAVE A CHOICE.

CHLOROFORM?

WHAT'S GOING ON HERE? WHERE AM I?

YOU'RE SAFE, LAURA. WE'RE IN A HOTEL IN LOWER MANHATTAN.

I'M NATHAN POLLACK WITH THE FEDERAL BUREAU OF INVESTIGATION.

FBI

F.B.I.? SINCE WHEN IS THE F.B.I. LICENSED TO ANAESTHETIZE PEOPLE?

GENE ROBILLARD, UNITED STATES SECRET SERVICE.

DID YOU KNOW THE MAN WALKING WITH YOU IN THE GARAGE?

DETECTIVE SULLIVAN? I JUST MET HIM TONIGHT. HE CAME TO TELL ME ABOUT--

ARI...

YOU COULD SAY THAT. CAN YOU PROVIDE US WITH ANY INFORMATION ABOUT IT?

I DON'T THINK SO. I'VE BEEN HERE IN NEW YORK.

WAIT. AM *I* A SUSPECT?

IT'S NOTHING LIKE THAT. WE'RE JUST TRYING TO--

ARE YOU WHO'S INVESTIGATING HIS MURDER?

WELL, THEN, AS MUCH AS I'D LIKE TO HELP, I DON'T *KNOW* WHAT HAPPENED TO ARI.

WE DON'T GET BADGES. IT'S MY CAFETERIA CARD.

TED WYCHEK, BUREAU OF CONSUMER ADVOCACY.

THAT'S GREAT, WYCHEK. YOU WANT TO SHOW HER YOUR PARKING PASS, TOO?

ANYWAY, MAYBE YOU *DO* KNOW SOMETHING, YOU JUST DON'T KNOW THAT YOU KNOW, YOU KNOW?

WHAT TED'S TRYING TO SAY IS, IF YOU TALK TO US, MAYBE WE CAN FIGURE THIS OUT TOGETHER.

LOOK... I'D FEEL BETTER IF I HAD SOMEONE WITH ME.

I WANT TO MAKE A PHONE CALL.

WE CAN'T LET YOU DO THAT.

YOU "CAN'T LET ME DO THAT?" I'LL TELL YOU WHAT YOU CAN'T DO. YOU CAN'T MAKE ME *STAY HERE.* YOU CERTAINLY CAN'T *DRUG* ME.

TAKE IT EASY.

NOT UNTIL I GET A *PHONE CALL.*

YOU NEED TO HELP US FIRST, THEN WE CAN TALK ABOUT A PHONE CALL.

HELP YOU WITH *WHAT?* I DON'T EVEN KNOW WHAT I'M DOING HERE.

YOU'RE HERE BECAUSE THE UNITED STATES GOVERNMENT MAY BE TRYING TO KILL YOU.

TWO

THREE COINS IN THE FOUNTAIN

THE TRUTH IS, WE WERE HOPING *YOU* COULD TELL *US* WHAT THEY WANT WITH YOU.

I STUDY DISEASES. WHO'D HAVE A PROBLEM WITH THAT?

YOU AND DR. MUSA ARE MIXED UP IN *SOMETHING*, EVEN IF YOU DON'T REALIZE IT.

IT'S A GOOD THING TED WAS WATCHING YOU.

MY TEAM PROFILES THE HIGH-RISK INDIVIDUALS THAT THE GOVERNMENT PLANS TO... NEUTRALIZE. WHEN THEY HAD US DO A TRAVEL SUMMARY ON YOU AND YOUR RESEARCH PARTNER, I TOOK YOU BOTH FOR SOME KIND OF SECURITY THREAT.

BUT YOU DIDN'T HAVE ANY FLAGS.

USUALLY THERE'S A *FLAG*-- A REASON THAT A PERSON WARRANTS ATTENTION.

AS FAR AS WE CAN TELL, THERE ISN'T A REASON FOR THE GOVERNMENT TO BE WATCHING *EITHER* OF YOU.

THAT CAUGHT *OUR* ATTENTION, SO WE STARTING KEEPING TABS ON THE TWO OF YOU. WHEN WE HEARD ABOUT MUSA'S MURDER, WE GUESSED YOU MIGHT BE NEXT.

IF YOU'D GOTTEN INTO THAT DETECTIVE'S CAR, ODDS ARE YOU NEVER WOULD'VE BEEN SEEN AGAIN.

AS FOR WHY THEY CHOSE TO MOVE ON YOUR PARTNER *FIRST*--

I'D LIKE TO SEE TONIGHT'S CHECK-IN SLIPS.

YEAH? WELL, I'D LIKE A *TWELVE-INCH--*

OH... UH... SORRY, OFFICER. LET ME GET THOSE FOR YOU.

I DIDN'T MEAN ANY, UH, DISRESPECT. IT'S JUST THAT WE GET A LOT OF, YOU KNOW, SHADY GUYS LOOKING FOR THEIR WIVES AND GIRLFRIENDS AND STUFF.

IS THERE A SPARE KEY FOR 206, OR AM I TAKING THE DOOR DOWN?

YOU CAN, UH, HAVE THE MASTER.

SHOULD I ASK TO, LIKE, SEE A *WARRANT* OR SOMETHING?

I JUST CHECK THE PEOPLE IN, YOU KNOW? ANYTHING *ILLEGAL* GOING ON UP THERE'S GOT NOTHING TO DO WITH ME!

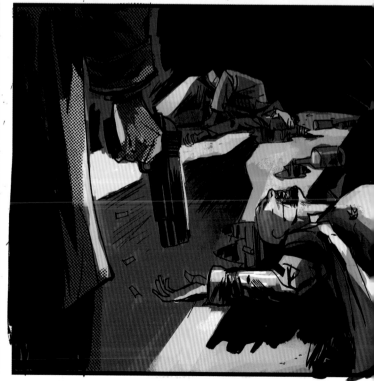

YOU *GOT RID* OF MY WALLET?

PEOPLE ARE LOOKING FOR YOU. CREDIT CARDS, DRIVER'S LICENSES...

... THESE THINGS LEAVE A TRAIL.

AND WHAT IF SOMEONE FINDS IT AND DECIDES TO MAX OUT MY CREDIT LIMIT? WHAT THEN?

OOPS.

YOU ABDUCT ME, STEAL MY PURSE, HOLD ME AGAINST MY WILL, AND NOW I'LL BE ARGUING WITH THE BANKS FOR MONTHS OVER FRAUDULENT CHARGES.

I'VE HAD ENOUGH. RELEASE ME, OR--

AM I ON *TV?*

--ASSAULTED A POLICE OFFICER EARLIER THIS EVENING, AND HAS SINCE DISAPPEARED.

THIS WOMAN IS WANTED FOR QUESTIONING IN THE MURDER OF AN ATLANTA MAN WHOSE BODY WAS FOUND THIS MORNING.

SHE IS FIVE FEET, SEVEN INCHES IN HEIGHT, WEIGHS ONE HUNDRED TWENTY POUNDS, AND HAS BROWN HAIR AND BROWN EYES.

SHE MAY BE TRAVELING WITH OTHERS.

IF YOU SEE HER, OR KNOW OF HER WHEREABOUTS, DO NOT ATTEMPT TO APPREHEND HER, BUT CALL YOUR LOCAL POLICE HOT-LINE IMMEDIATELY.

WE'RE *DEFINITELY* ON TO SOMETHING HERE.

CLASSIC STAGE-ONE DISINFORMATION. THEY'RE NOT GOING ALL-OUT, THOUGH. WE STILL HAVE TIME.

JUST DISGRUNTLED EMPLOYEES WHO DON'T LIKE THE WAY THEIR COMPANY DOES BUSINESS. IF IT WASN'T FOR THE INTERAGENCY MANDATE OF THE PATRIOT ACT, WE PROBABLY NEVER WOULD'VE MET.

WHO *ARE* YOU GUYS?

IRONIC, RIGHT?

YOU HAVE TO TRUST SOMEONE, DOCTOR. SO WHO'S IT GOING TO BE?

ST. ANNE HOSPITAL,
NEW YORK CITY.

DR. LASKY?

WHAT IS IT, GRACE?

TWO CASES OF RESPIRATORY DISTRESS WERE ADMITTED THROUGH THE EMERGENCY ROOM OF ST. FRANCIS HOSPITAL IN BOSTON.

THE PATIENTS DIDN'T RESPOND TO TREATMENT, AND BOTH ARE NOW CRITICAL.

THEIR DOCTORS THINK IT'S A BACTERIOLOGICAL INFECTION, BUT THEY CAN'T IDENTIFY IT.

THEY THINK THEY'VE GOT A NEW DISEASE.

IT SAYS HERE THAT A THIRD CASE WAS ADMITTED AT A DIFFERENT BOSTON HOSPITAL. IT SAYS THAT THEY HAVEN'T BEEN ABLE TO ESTABLISH A LINK BETWEEN THE THREE PATIENTS.

OH, YEAH. AND IN FEBRUARY '09, SHE BOUGHT LINGERIE FROM AN ONLINE CATALOGUE BASED IN WHITE PLAINS.

IF YOU WANT TO KNOW WHO HER VALENTINE'S DATE WAS, I'VE GOT HIS PASSPORT PHOTO.

I'LL PASS. WHAT ABOUT FRIENDS AND FAMILY? ANY LINKS THERE?

I'M WORKING ON THE THIRD GENERATION NOW. DIG DEEP ENOUGH, AND EVERYONE'S LIFE PASSES THROUGH THE BIG APPLE AT SOME POINT, BUT I'M NOT SEEING ANY FLAGS.

WHAT *DO* WE HAVE?

THERE'S ONE LEAD, BUT IT'S IFFY. AND WE'LL ONLY GET ONE CHANCE TO USE IT.

MAYBE.

I'LL TAKE WHAT I CAN GET. ANYTHING IS BETTER THAN GOING BACK TO HOMESEC EMPTY-HANDED.

OH, THEY'RE GOING TO *LOVE* THIS.

BLONDE HAIR, THRIFT-STORE CLOTHES... IT'S A WHOLE NEW ME.

WHERE IS EVERYBODY?

THEY'RE GETTING TAKEOUT. HOPE YOU LIKE CHINESE.

I'LL SETTLE FOR ANYTHING. ALL THIS RUNNING AROUND HAS MY EATING SCHEDULE OUT OF WHACK. MY BLOOD SUGAR IS DOING BACKFLIPS.

...IT'S NOT POLITE TO STARE.

MY TRAINED PHYSICIAN'S EYE SEES A SERIOUS CASE OF *CARPAL TUNNEL* IN YOUR FUTURE. WHAT ARE LOOKING FOR ON THAT THING, ANYWAY?

A CLUE AS TO WHY THE GOVERNMENT IS SO INTERESTED IN YOU.

SO FAR, THERE'S JUST COVER STORIES ABOUT YOU MURDERING YOUR "LOVER" IN ATLANTA.

YOU SAID THERE'S STILL TIME BECAUSE THEY HAVEN'T GONE "ALL OUT." WHAT'D YOU MEAN BY THAT?

WE'LL KNOW THEY'VE EXHAUSTED ALL OF THEIR OPTIONS WHEN THEY MENTION THE KIDS.

IT'S *ALWAYS* ABOUT THE KIDS.

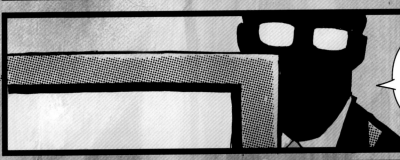

OUTLAW GUNS SO TIMMY DOESN'T SHOOT HIMSELF. BAN BOOKS SO JANIE DOESN'T GET ANY WRONG IDEAS. CENSOR CYBERSPACE SO JOHNNY DOESN'T STUMBLE UPON ANY TITS AND--

YOU GET THE POINT. WHENEVER THEY START TALKING ABOUT THE KIDS, YOU KNOW THEY'RE FOR REAL.

BUT FOR THE TIME BEING, THEY'RE PLAYING IT MORE LOW-KEY. THEY RELEASED A POLICE SKETCH, BUT NOT YOUR PHOTO. THEY GAVE OUT YOUR HEIGHT AND WEIGHT, BUT NOT YOUR NAME.

THEY'RE TRYING TO SCARE YOU INTO MAKING A MISTAKE, SO THEY CAN FIND YOU AND BRING YOU IN ON THEIR OWN. KEEP THINGS QUIET.

FIND ME? *I'M* NOT EVEN SURE WHERE I AM.

WHEN THEY'RE FINISHED, THEY'LL KNOW MORE ABOUT YOU THAN *YOU* DO. AND THEY'LL USE THAT KNOWLEDGE TO SNIFF YOU OUT.

YOU'RE ONE OF THOSE *TINFOIL-HAT* TYPES, AREN'T YOU?

TOMMY LORENZO, BRENDA GILLETTE, AND JULIE DONOVAN.

WHAT?

YOUR PROM DATE, COLLEGE ROOMATE, AND COFFEEHOUSE FRIEND. WHAT THEY DON'T KNOW AT BOCA IS THAT SOMEONE *ALREADY DID* YOUR PROFILE.

I HAD TO BE SURE YOU WEREN'T WORKING WITH THEM.

SO WHAT DO WE DO?

THE ONLY THING WE CAN-- TRY TO FIND OUT WHY THEY'RE AFTER YOU AND *EXPOSE* THEM.

AS FOR HIDING FROM THEM...

...NO MATTER HOW CAREFUL YOU ARE, NO MATTER HOW WELL YOU THINK YOU'VE COVERED YOUR TRACKS--

-- THEY'LL DIG UP SOMETHING. WE *ALWAYS* DO.

THREE
CASH
CRISIS

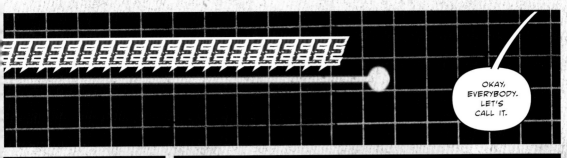

OKAY, EVERYBODY. LET'S CALL IT.

PATIENT EXPIRED AT 7:47 A.M.

ANYONE SEEN HIS MOTHER? I NEED TO LET HER KNOW.

SHE'S ASLEEP IN THE WAITING ROOM.

LET'S GET SITUATED IN HERE BEFORE WE--

DR. LASKY?

THERE'S TWO PATIENTS IN ADMITTING, BOTH COMPLAINING ABOUT COUGHING AND LABORED BREATHING. IT LOOKS LIKE P.D.S.

THAT'S FIVE NEW CASES SINCE LAST NIGHT.

CAN SOMEBODY PLEASE TELL ME WHAT THE HELL IS GOING ON HERE?

WHAT ARE YOU DOING?

CHECKING MY E-MAIL?

NOT HERE, YOU'RE NOT. NOT FROM *MY* LAPTOP.

HE'S RIGHT. THEY'LL BE MONITORING YOUR ACCOUNT TO SEE WHERE YOU ACCESS IT FROM. IF THEY GET A FIX ON THE LAPTOP'S IP ADDRESS, THEY'LL BE ABLE TO FIND OUT WHAT WEBSITES IT'S VISITED, WHO IT'S CHATTED WITH, *EVERYTHING.*

IT'LL TAKE BOCA ALL OF TWO SECONDS TO CONNECT IT TO ME.

WHAT, THEN?

THERE'S AN INTERNET CAFÉ THREE BLOCKS AWAY. YOU CAN LOG IN FROM THERE, BUT YOU'LL HAVE TO BE QUICK ABOUT IT.

HOW QUICK?

FROM THE SECOND YOU LOG IN UNTIL THE COPS SHOW UP? FIVE MINUTES, TOPS.

"SECRETARY KEENE IS HERE, MR. PRESIDENT."

"THANK YOU, DORIS. SHOW HIM IN."

YES, WELL, THERE'VE BEEN SOME DEVELOPMENTS THAT MERIT OUR *IMMEDIATE* ATTENTION.

ANDERS, WHY DON'T YOU BRING ALBERT UP TO SPEED.

GOOD. THEN YOU'RE AWARE THAT IT'S REPORTING THE OUTBREAK OF AN UNIDENTIFIED RESPIRATORY ILLNESS IN BOSTON.

EARLIER TODAY I SPOKE WITH BOB EVERETT AT THE C.D.C. HE SAYS BOSTON ISN'T ALONE. CASES OF THIS MYSTERY SICKNESS HAVE POPPED UP IN SEVERAL METROPOLITAN AREAS.

WHY DIDN'T I HEAR ABOUT THIS FROM YOUR OFFICE?

WE'RE LOOKING INTO IT, MR. PRESIDENT, BUT THERE'S NOTHING TO MAKE US THINK THAT THIS FALLS UNDER *HOMESEC*'S PURVIEW.

THANK YOU FOR COMING ON SUCH SHORT NOTICE, ALBERT.

OF COURSE, MR. PRESIDENT, THOUGH I DIDN'T EXPECT TO BE BACK UNTIL OUR APPOINTMENT LATER IN THE WEEK.

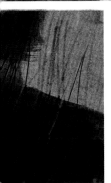

THIS IS A COPY OF THE MOST RECENT MORBIDITY AND MORTALITY WEEKLY REPORT. IT'S A NEWSLETTER--

I AM *FAMILIAR* WITH THE M.M.W.R. MY STAFF AND I REVIEW IT *EVERY* WEEK.

WHEN I INVITED YOU TO STAY ON FROM THE PREVIOUS ADMINISTRATION, WHAT WAS IT THAT I SAID TO YOU?

THAT YOU DIDN'T CARE ABOUT PARTY POLITICS. YOU WANTED THE BEST MAN FOR THE JOB.

IS THAT STILL YOU?

YES, MR. PRESIDENT.

THEN QUIT PLAYING IT SAFE AND TELL ME WHAT'S ON YOUR MIND.

A FEW DAYS AGO, A RESEARCHER AT C.D.C. WAS MURDERED.

INVESTIGATORS SUSPECT HIS COLLEAGUE-- A DR. LAURA REGAN-- BUT HAVE BEEN UNABLE TO LOCATE HER.

REGAN EARNED HER REPUTATION WORKING ON THE TOUGHEST BUGS OUT THERE. SHE HAS THE KEYS TO THE FREEZER, AND IT WAS SOON AFTER HER DISAPPEARANCE THAT CASES OF THE RESPIRATORY ILLNESS BEGAN SURFACING.

WHILE IT WOULD BE PREMATURE TO CONCLUDE THAT THESE EVENTS ARE RELATED, AT THE VERY LEAST WE SHOULD CONSIDER THE POSSIBILITY THAT DR. REGAN IS SOMEHOW INVOLVED WITH THE OUTBREAK.

I DON'T KNOW ABOUT YOU, MR. PRESIDENT, BUT IT SOUNDS TO *ME* LIKE THIS FALLS UNDER HOMESEC'S PURVIEW.

I AGREE.

I HAVE TO SAY, ALBERT, YOUR SLOWNESS TO ACTION ON THIS IS TROUBLING. I THOUGHT ANDERS CONVEYED MY POSITION AT OUR LAST MEETING, BUT IN CASE THERE WAS SOME CONFUSION, I'LL REITERATE.

AMERICA MAY BE A TARGET OF TERROR, BUT THIS ISN'T ISRAEL. OUR CITIZENS WILL NEVER ACCEPT DOWNED AIRLINERS AND HOMICIDE BOMBERS AS A WAY OF LIFE.

THE ONLY ACCEPTABLE CIVILIAN LOSSES ARE *ZERO* LOSSES.

BOCA HAS A LEAD ON THE DOCTOR, AND ONCE WE BRING HER IN WE WILL BE BETTER ABLE TO DETERMINE--

AS A RESULT OF 9/11, YOU'VE BEEN GIVEN THE RARE LUXURY OF HEADING AN AGENCY WITH ALL OF ITS ADMINSTRATIVE, BUDGETARY, AND LEGAL NEEDS SATISFIED.

NOW, I SUGGEST YOU TAKE ADVANTAGE OF THAT GOOD FORTUNE--

"--AND GIVE THE PEOPLE THE *PERFECTION* THEY'RE ASKING FOR."

YOUR DRIVER SAID I'D FIND YOU HERE. IS EVERYTHING ALL RIGHT?

WALK WITH ME.

HOW CAN A MAN BE ELECTED PRESIDENT OF THE MOST POWERFUL NATION ON EARTH, YET BE SO NAÏVE AS TO HOW GOVERNMENT OPERATES?

I GATHER THE MEETING DIDN'T GO WELL.

"SECURITY."

HE SAYS THE WORD LIKE AN INCANTATION, AS THOUGH MERELY SPEAKING IT ALOUD WILL CONJURE IT FROM THE ETHER.

HE HAS NO INKLING OF WHAT IT TAKES TO PROTECT A NATION.

TO BE SUCCESSFUL, A POLITICIAN DOESN'T NEED TO *BE* AN EFFECTIVE LEADER. HE JUST HAS TO *LOOK* LIKE ONE.

HE'S GOTTEN WORD OF THE ILLNESS, THEN?

EVERETT CONTACTED HIM.

WE COULD LEAK A COVER STORY. TELL THE PRESS THAT THE TERRORISTS HAVE A SUPERBUG, AND THAT ONE OF C.D.C.'S OWN HELPED THEM ACQUIRE IT.

EVERETT WOULD HAVE A HARD TIME EXPLAINING HIS WAY OUT OF THAT, AND THE PRESIDENT COULDN'T HELP BUT THROW HIS ARMS AROUND HOMESEC.

NO. EVEN IF LAURA REGAN WAS NOT COMPLICATING MATTERS, THERE IS A *LARGER* CONCERN.

OVER THREE THOUSAND CITIZENS DIED ON 9/11, BUT IT TOOK ONLY DAYS FOR PASSENGERS TO START BOARDING PLANES AGAIN.

THE DAMAGE FROM THE ATTACK FADED LIKE A BRUISE.

BUT WHAT IF THE NUMBER LOST THAT DAY WAS *FIVE HUNDRED* THOUSAND? OR *ONE MILLION?*

A NUMBER SO LARGE THAT THE BIGGEST CITIES AND THE SMALLEST TOWNS FELT ITS SIGNIFICANCE. THEN MAYBE THE COUNTRY WOULD HAVE CHANGED ITS WAYS FOREVER.

SO WHAT CHOICE DO WE HAVE BUT TO WAIT?

WHEN WE FINALLY TELL THE PEOPLE WHAT MADE THEM ILL, THE WOUND MUST BE SO DEEP THAT IT LEAVES A *SCAR.*

BECAUSE IF SIX WEEKS AFTER ALL OF THIS IS OVER EVERYTHING RETURNS TO THE WAY IT WAS, WHAT WILL WE HAVE GAINED?

RESOLVE, ELLIOT. CHOOSING A COURSE OF ACTION THAT SERVES THE GREATER GOOD—NO MATTER HOW DIFFICULT A COURSE IT MAY BE—AND COMMITTING TO IT.

POLLSTERS AND BIOGRAPHERS BE DAMNED.

THAT IS THE STUFF OF LEADERS.

PDS IN MINNEAPOLIS?

Regarding the article in the current MMWR. I'm with the Minneapolis DOH, and I've been monitoring several patients with symptoms ...m to match.

tap
tap
tap

tap
tap
tap

tap

BUT THE EPIDEMIOLOGY DOESN'T MAKE SENSE. USUALLY THERE'S A PATTERN TO THE WAY AN ILLNESS SPREADS. METHODS OF CONTRACTION, INCUBATION PERIODS, SYMPTOMS OF INFECTION--

-- THEY CAN MAKE THE PATTERN HARD TO SEE, BUT THE PATTERN IS *ALWAYS* THERE.

IT'S LIKE BUILDING A PROFILE AT BOCA.

IT COMES DOWN TO FINDING WHEN AND WHERE PEOPLE CROSS PATHS.

BUT THESE CASES ARE SO SCATTERED, IT'S HARD TO TELL WHERE *ANY* OF THE PATIENTS CROSSED PATHS.

THAT'S NOT GOOD.

WHAT ABOUT INFECTED TRAVELERS?

MAYBE, BUT THEN THE CASES WOULD BE CLUSTERED AROUND BIG HUBS LIKE MIAMI AND LOS ANGELES.

INSTEAD, THEY'RE POPPING UP IN PLACES LIKE KANSAS CITY AND RICHMOND.

DID YOU SAY RICHMOND?

WHAT ARE SOME OF THE OTHER CITIES?

THERE'S BOSTON, CLEVELAND, MINNEAPOLIS...

DAMN.

FOUR
DIRTY MONEY

SAN FRANCISCO.

DALLAS.

KANSAS CITY.

MINNEAPOLIS.

OH, GOD...

I'VE BEEN CARRYING AROUND A *GERM FACTORY!*

WHAT'RE YOU GIVING IT TO *ME* FOR?!?

THERE'S NO SENSE WORRYING WHICH OF US HAS BEEN EXPOSED. IF THERE'S ANYTHING CATCHABLE IN THIS BAG--

-- THEN *ALL* OF US HAVE ALREADY CAUGHT IT.

HOW CAN WE TELL? WOULD I FEEL HOT? BECAUSE I THINK I'VE BEEN FEELING HOT LATELY.

JUDGING BY HOW MUCH YOU SWEAT, I'D WAGER THAT YOU *ALWAYS* FEEL HOT.

GO ON AND MAKE JOKES, BUT THIS IS *SERIOUS*. WE COULD ALL BE COMING DOWN WITH...

WHAT *WOULD* WE BE COMING DOWN WITH, ANYWAY?

IT'S SOME KIND OF RESPIRATORY INFECTION. THAT'S ALL I HAD TIME TO GLEAN FROM THE E-MAILS, BESIDES THAT IT'S ON THE VERGE OF BECOMING AN *EPIDEMIC*.

THE ONLY WAY TO KNOW MORE IS IF I CAN SEE THE BUG FIRSTHAND.

WE CAN'T EXACLY START BANGING ON HOSPITAL DOORS AND ASKING IF ANY OF THEIR PATIENTS ARE *REALLY SICK*.

WE WOULDN'T EVEN KNOW WHERE TO START.

TURN AROUND.

WE HAVE TO GO BACK.

BACK WHERE? BACK *THERE?*

WE CAN'T GO BACK THERE!

I HATE TO SAY IT, BUT WYCHEK IS RIGHT. WE DIDN'T GET CAUGHT, BUT THAT EMAIL STUNT CONFIRMED WE WERE IN THE CITY. THAT'S WHERE THEY'LL CONCENTRATE THEIR RESOURCES NOW.

SAFEST PLACE FOR US IS ANY-WHERE ELSE.

THAT MAY BE, BUT IT DOESN'T CHANGE THE FACT THAT WE HAVE TO GO BACK.

IF THE GOVERNMENT WANTS ME DEAD, THEN IT'S BECAUSE I POSE SOME SORT OF THREAT TO THEIR PLANS.

I WON'T KNOW WHY OR HOW UNTIL I'VE HAD A CHANCE TO EXAMINE SOME CULTURES, AND I THINK THERE'S A PLACE IN THE CITY WHERE I CAN DO JUST THAT.

ACTUALLY, GOING BACK MIGHT NOT BE SUCH A BAD IDEA...

I'M NOT RELISHING THE IDEA OF CASHING IN MORE *WIRE TRANSFERS.*

SO UNLESS WE COME UP WITH ANOTHER METHOD OF PAYMENT, OUR OPTIONS ARE LIMITED TO HOW FAR WE CAN MAKE IT ON THIS TANK OF GAS.

IT'S TIME WE PAID A VISIT TO OUR VENTURE CAPITALIST.

YOU'RE NOT SERIOUS.

THAT'S CRAZY!

GENE, TELL HIM HE'S CRAZY!

THINK OF IT THIS WAY, TED: IN THE UNFORTUNATE EVENT THAT YOUR DAMPNESS ISN'T DUE TO YOUR USUAL RATE OF PERSPIRATION, LAURA IS THE PERSON WITH THE BEST CHANCE OF CURING YOU.

YOU THINK SHE CAN DO THAT FROM SOME RUN-DOWN MOTEL IN BUFFALO?

IF YOU'VE GOT A BETTER WAY TO COVER OUR OPERATING EXPENSES, I'D LOVE TO HEAR IT.

THE CITY MIGHT NOT BE SUCH A BAD IDEA.

WAY TO STICK TO YOUR GUNS.

ALRIGHT, BUT WE'RE GOING TO DO THINGS MY WAY. THAT MEANS WE MAKE YOUR STOP FIRST, POLLACK.

IN THE MEANTIME, DOCTOR, WHY DON'T YOU TELL ME WHAT YOU HAVE IN MIND.

I PUT MY BEST TEAM ON IT, BUT THERE'S ONLY SO MUCH THEY CAN DO WHEN THEY'RE A MAN SHORT.

A MAN SHORT?

TED WYCHEK. HE'S ONE OF MY TOP CRUNCHERS, BUT HE'S OUT OF TOWN AT HIS UNCLE'S FUNERAL.

AND HE WAS ONE OF THE MEN ASSIGNED TO LAURA REGAN?

HE HELPED PUT TOGETHER THE TRAVEL SUMMARY YOU ORDERED.

I SEE.

REGAN'S ABILITY TO VANISH AFTER LEAVING SUCH AN EXTENSIVE RECORD OF HER LIFE IN YOUR DATABANKS-- WOULD YOU DESCRIBE THAT AS *TYPICAL?*

OR WOULD YOU SAY THAT, IN ALL LIKELIHOOD, SHE'S BEING ASSISTED BY SOMEONE WITH AN INTIMATE KNOWLEDGE OF YOUR RESEARCH AND TRACKING METHODS?

AN *INSIDER'S* KNOWLEDGE, YOU MIGHT SAY.

UH...

LET ME ASK YOU THIS:

DO YOU EVEN KNOW IF THIS WYCHEK *HAS* AN UNCLE?

ST. LOUIS.

CHICAGO.

ATLANTA.

RICHMOND.

CALL.

"THAT'S A FLUSH, BOYS."

LUCKY BASTARD.

CHOKE ON IT.

DEAL ME OUT.

YOU WANT US TO GO WITH YOU, BOSS?

NAH. SALLIE AND LOU-LOU CAN HANDLE IT.

WELL, IF THIS AIN'T A MOTLEY LOOKING BUNCH.

NO, DON'T TELL ME. I WANT TO GUESS.

YOU'VE GOT GAMBLING DEBTS COMING OUT OF YOUR EARS. I'D SAY *INTERNET*, BY THE LOOKS OF YOU.

YOU'RE THE *WIFE*, BUT YOU'RE TIRED OF BEING MARRIED TO A DEGENERATE, SO YOU'RE STEPPING OUT WITH THIS ONE HERE.

BUT HE WANTS TO START COMING IN THROUGH THE *FRONT* DOOR--

-- SO HE HIRED *MR. SERIOUS* BACK THERE TO PUT HUBBY IN THE GROUND.

HOW'D I DO?

I'M WITH THE *SECRET SERVICE*.

THEY'RE *C.D.C.*, *F.B.I.*, AND *BOCA*, RESPECTIVELY.

THAT'S A LOTTA ALPHABET.

WE'RE NOT HERE AS PART OF ANY INVESTIGATION. WE JUST WANT TO TALK.

OH, YOU JUST WANT TO *TALK*. SIT AROUND AND CHEW THE FAT LIKE WE'RE PALS.

LOU-LOU, WHY DON'T YOU SEE IF OUR *PALS* HERE WOULD LIKE SOME REFRESHMENTS.

ACTUALLY, I COULD USE A, UH...

NEVERMIND.

WE DON'T HAVE TO BE PALS TO BE BUSINESS PARTNERS.

I'VE SEEN YOU SOMEPLACE.

YEAH. YOU'RE THE FED PENCIL PUSHER THAT HELPED PUT MY *BABY BROTHER* AWAY. DOMMIE'S GOT SEVEN YEARS LEFT ON A *TEN-YEAR BIT* BECAUSE OF YOU.

YOU GOT SOME SET COMING AROUND *THIS* NEIGHBORHOOD.

FORGET ABOUT YOUR BADGES. THE FAMILY MAN IN ME WANTS TO SHOW YOU WHAT HAPPENS TO PEOPLE WHO TESTIFY AGAINST US.

AND SHOW YOU *SLOWLY.*

OR YOU COULD FIND OUT WHAT YOU HAVE TO *GAIN* FROM A GROUP OF FEDERAL AGENTS THAT NEED YOUR HELP.

BUSINESS PARTNERS, YOU SAY?

ALRIGHT THEN. LET'S HAVE A SEAT AND LISTEN TO YOUR PROPOSITION.

IF THAT'S NOT A GOOD ENOUGH REASON FOR YOU, CONSIDER THAT IN A CASHLESS ECONOMY, PEOPLE IN YOUR LINE OF WORK--

... WILL FIND IT A LOT HARDER TO DO BUSINESS.

WHAT ABOUT YOU, LITTLE LADY? YOU'RE WHO'S GOING TO SAVE THE DAY.

MAYBE...

YOU KNOW WHAT I CAN'T FIGURE?

YOU TESTIFIED THAT THERE WAS TWO HUNDRED GRAND IN THE SAFE WHEN THE FEDS RAIDED DOMMIE'S CLUB, BUT HE SWEARS THE NUMBER WAS CLOSER TO *THREE* HUNDRED.

YOU WOULDN'T KNOW ANYTHING ABOUT *THAT*, WOULD YOU?

CLEVELAND.

PHILADELPHIA.

BOSTON.

NEW YORK CITY.

JESUS, WHERE HAVE YOU BEEN? I'VE BEEN TRYING TO GET IN TOUCH WITH YOU FOR DAYS.

YOU DIDN'T SEE ME ON THE NEWS?

THAT'S YOU? I MEAN, I KNOW IT LOOKS LIKE YOU, BUT THE STUFF THEY'RE SAYING...

I DIDN'T HURT ANYONE, RON.

YOU DON'T NEED TO TELL ME THAT. WE'VE KNOWN EACH OTHER TOO LONG.

HAVE YOU HEARD ABOUT WHAT'S GOING ON?

THAT'S WHY WE'RE HERE.

DO YOU REMEMBER THE PATIENT YOU TOLD ME ABOUT AT THE BANQUET?

REGGIE WALTERS. HE DIDN'T MAKE IT.

IS YOUR OFFER TO SHOW ME HIS CULTURES STILL GOOD?

I'VE GOT EVERYTHING IN MY LAB.

ANY WAY YOU CAN GET US UP THERE?

THERE'S A SERVICE ELEVATOR AROUND BACK. MEET ME THERE IN TEN MINUTES, AND I'LL SEE WHAT I CAN COME UP WITH.

THANKS FOR TRUSTING ME, RON.

HEY, IT'S LIKE I ALWAYS SAY--

-- HELP FROM A FUGITIVE IS BETTER THAN NO HELP AT ALL.

ONCE AGAIN, WE ARE RECEIVING REPORTS FROM AREA HOSPITALS ABOUT AN OUTBREAK OF SOME UNDETERMINED ILLNESS.

IF YOU ARE EXPERIENCING HIGH FEVER, TROUBLE BREATHING, OR ANY OTHER PNEUMONIA-LIKE SYMPTOMS, YOU SHOULD VISIT A HEALTHCARE PROFESSIONAL IMMEDIATELY.

MOM? IT'S TEDDY. ARE YOU OKAY?

NOW WE INTERRUPT THIS STORY TO BRING YOU MORE BREAKING NEWS...

I NEED YOU TO CALL THE BANK AND TELL THEM YOU WON'T BE COMING TO WORK FOR A FEW DAYS.

POLICE HAVE IDENTIFIED THE WOMAN THEY SAY IS RESPONSIBLE FOR THE MURDER OF HER COWORKER IN ATLANTA.

NO, I CAN'T EXPLAIN RIGHT NOW. JUST *DO THIS* FOR ME, WILL YOU?

HER NAME IS LAURA REGAN, AND SHE WAS LAST SEEN IN THE MANHATTAN AREA.

POLICE BELIEVE SHE HAS ABDUCTED A YOUNG BOY AND IS HOLDING HIM HOSTAGE. AN AMBER ALERT HAS BEEN ISSUED FOR THE TRI-STATE AREA.

NOT THE KIDS...

POLICE ASK THAT YOU BE ON THE LOOKOUT...

NOTHING, MOM. I HAVE TO GO.

FIVE
BUYING
POWER

SAN FRANCISCO.

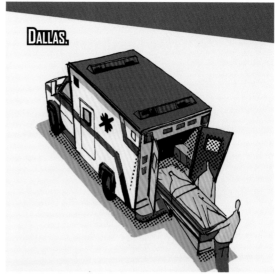

DALLAS.

KANSAS CITY.

MINNEAPOLIS.

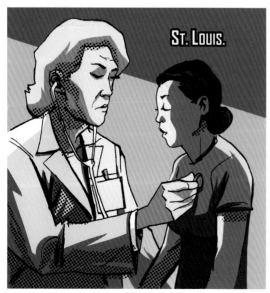

ST. LOUIS.

CHICAGO.

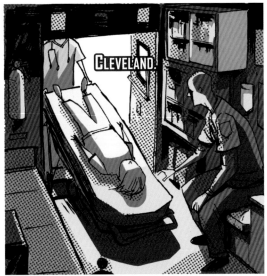

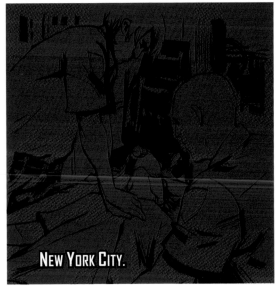

SIX YEARS AGO, ARI AND I WERE PART OF A CLASSIFIED PROJECT.

THE WORK WAS GRUELING, BUT IT WAS AN OPPORTUNITY TO STUDY SOMETHING NEW.

IT WAS A WEAPONIZED BACTERIUM STRAIGHT FROM THE U.S.S.R.'S *CHEM-BIO* PROGRAM.

THE FORMER SOVIET BLOC WAS IN A SHAMBLES, AND THE INTELLIGENCE AGENCIES KNEW THERE WAS A GROWING *BLACK MARKET* FOR THEIR MILITARY TECHNOLOGIES.

THE FEAR WAS THAT THE BACTERIUM WOULD BE SMUGGLED OUT OF THE LABS AND SOLD TO THE HIGHEST BIDDER. AFTER ALL, WE'D MANAGED TO GET *OUR* HANDS ON IT.

THE PROJECT LEADERS WANTED A VACCINE STOCKPILED TO PROTECT AGAINST THAT POSSIBILTY, AND WE COULD SEE WHY. ONCE INFECTED, THE *DEATH RATE* IN OUR TEST ANIMALS WAS OVER NINETY PERCENT.

WE NAMED THE BACTERIUM "ZORRO" BECAUSE OF ITS Z-SHAPED STRUCTURE. AND BECAUSE IT ALWAYS LEFT ITS MARK.

IT TOOK US MORE THAN A YEAR, BUT WE FINALLY CRACKED IT.

THEY THANKED US FOR OUR TIME AND SENT US ON OUR WAY.

HOW IS IT CONTRACTED?

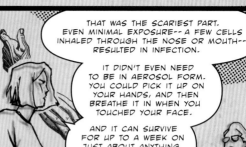

THAT WAS THE SCARIEST PART. EVEN MINIMAL EXPOSURE-- A FEW CELLS INHALED THROUGH THE NOSE OR MOUTH-- RESULTED IN INFECTION.

IT DIDN'T EVEN NEED TO BE IN AEROSOL FORM. YOU COULD PICK IT UP ON YOUR HANDS, AND THEN BREATHE IT IN WHEN YOU TOUCHED YOUR FACE.

AND IT CAN SURVIVE FOR UP TO A WEEK ON JUST ABOUT ANYTHING. PHONES, LAPTOPS, DOORKNOBS...

MONEY.

EVEN MONEY.

I'M SORRY. DID YOU JUST SAY MONEY?

LAURA, WHAT'S GOING ON HERE? WHAT AM I NOT BEING TOLD?

IT'S THE PERFECT TACTICAL ORGANISM. IT'S NOT CONTAGIOUS, WHICH ALLOWS YOU TO MANAGE THE IMPACT. INSTEAD OF A WILDFIRE, YOU GET A *CONTROLLED BURN.*

THE GOOD NEWS IS THAT YOU *DID* CREATE A VACCINE.

AND THEY CAN KEEP PUTTING IT INTO CIRCULATION UNTIL THE DEATH TOLL IS HIGH ENOUGH TO SCARE PEOPLE OFF CASH FOREVER.

"-- AND LAURA REGAN IS ALL OUT OF BORROWED TIME."

LAURA REGAN, IF YOU CAN HEAR THIS, PLEASE BRING OUR SON HOME.

THAT HEARTFELT PLEA WAS ISSUED JUST MINUTES AGO BY THE MOTHER OF A BOY WHO WAS ABDUCTED EARLIER THIS EVENING.

WATCHING THAT ISN'T GOING TO DO YOU ANY GOOD.

THE IMAGINARY KID THAT I IMAGINARILY KIDNAPPED HAS A *MOM?*

OUR FRIENDS WILL BE IN D.C. BY MORNING.

YOU'RE SURE THEY'LL FIND THE TARGET AT THE HOTEL?

I'M SURE HE'S BEEN THERE EVERY THURSDAY FOR THE LAST SIX MONTHS.

THE ROOM IS ALWAYS REGISTERED IN THE INTERN'S NAME, OF COURSE.

SHOULD I EVEN ASK HOW YOU KNOW THIS?

SOMETIMES WE PROFILE PEOPLE JUST FOR FUN.

I KNOW LOTS OF *THINGS* ABOUT LOTS OF *PEOPLE.*

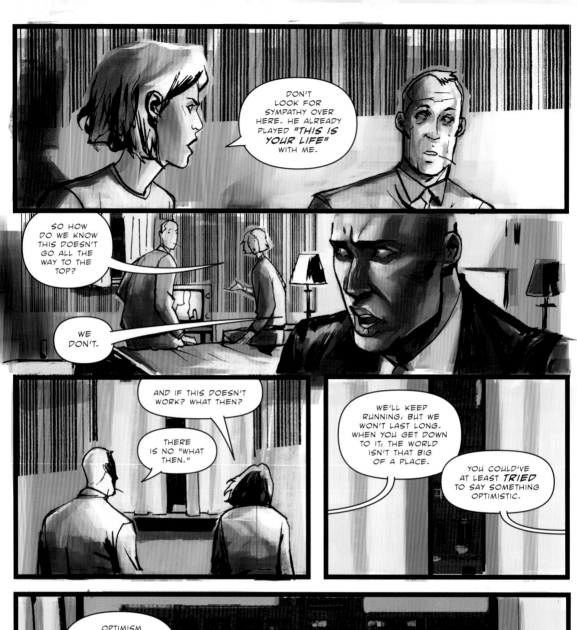

WASHINGTON, D.C.

WAS THAT ROOM SERVICE AT THE DOOR? YOU KNOW HOW I GET WHEN I DON'T EAT BEFORE THE MORNING BRIEFINGS.

HOW DOES IT LOOK?

I'VE SEEN *BETTER*.

YOUR LADY-FRIEND DECIDED TO TAKE A WALK, ANDERS.

IT'D BE A SIN TO LET THIS MEAL GO TO WASTE.

I WISH, JUST ONCE, WE COULD STAY IN ONE PLACE FOR MORE THAN EIGHT HOURS.

NOT UNTIL WE KNOW IF OUR MESSAGE GOT THROUGH.

WHAT'S WRONG, GENE?

POLLACK, PUT DOWN THE BAGS.

WHAT?

HOW WILL WE KNOW WHEN THAT HAPPENS?

BEST CASE? WE HEAR ABOUT IT ON THE NEWS.

WORST CASE, THEY SEND SOMEONE TO TELL US *IN PERSON.*

RUN!

LOOKS LIKE YOUR FRIEND'S CLOCK RUNS A LITTLE *FAST,* DOCTOR.

RON WOULDN'T GO BACK ON HIS WORD.

I MAY HAVE CALLED MY MOM FROM THE HOSPITAL.

WE HAVEN'T GIVEN THE NUMBER TO ANYONE ELSE.

THEN THEY MUST'VE GOTTEN IT FROM HIM SOMEHOW.

IF HE DIDN'T CONTACT THE AUTHORITIES, HOW DID THEY KNOW WE'D BEEN TO SEE HIM?

SHE'S A *BANK TELLER.* I COULDN'T JUST LET HER GO TO WORK!

BLAM

CAN WE MOVE HIM AGAIN?

I DON'T KNOW, HE'S LOST A LOT OF BLOOD...

I GUESS YOU'D BETTER *STAY PUT*, THEN.

YOU, PUT DOWN THE WEAPON.

DEET DEET DEET

GO AHEAD.

SIR?

THEY'RE RIGHT IN FRONT OF ME.

I COULD SAY THAT I ADMIRE YOU FOR MANAGING TO STAY ALIVE AS LONG AS YOU DID--

-- BUT THE TRUTH IS, I LIKE IT BETTER WHEN THE JOBS COME *EASY.*

EXCELLENT WORK. NOW, LET THEM GO.

SAY AGAIN?

YOU'RE TAKING ORDERS FROM *ME* NOW, AND I WANT YOU TO *LET THEM GO.*

I WON'T SAY IT A THIRD TIME.

LOOKS LIKE YOU'VE ALL BEEN GIVEN A **PRESIDENTIAL PARDON.**

I'LL TAKE CARE OF THE BODIES.

YOU CALL YOUR FRIEND AN AMBULANCE.

WHAT JUST HAPPENED?

I GUESS OUR MESSAGE GOT THROUGH.

EPILOGUE
THE WORLD
GOES 'ROUND

48 HOURS LATER.

HE LIVES.

NOW I KNOW HOW YOU FELT, DOCTOR.

I DIDN'T GET SHOT AND LOSE *SIX PINTS OF BLOOD*, SO I THINK YOU HAVE ME BEAT THERE.

CHLOROFORM DOES SEEM A LITTLE LESS RUDE.

SINCE WE'RE ALL STILL BREATHING, I ASSUME THE THREAT HAS PASSED?

THE ONLY WIDESPREAD MEDICAL COMPLAINT DOCTORS ARE GOING TO BE HEARING ABOUT IS A *BRUISED SHOULDER*.

NO WORD YET ON HOW MANY PATIENTS DIDN'T MAKE IT, BUT WE THINK IT'S LESS THAN A HUNDRED NATION-WIDE.

WHAT'S THE PARTY LINE?

THEY'RE SAYING THE OUTBREAK WAS CAUSED BY A NEW STRAIN OF PNEUMONIA THAT TRAVELS THROUGH AIR-CONDITIONING DUCTS. DESIGNATED "SICK BUILDINGS" IN TWELVE MAJOR CITIES ARE BEING DECONTAMINATED.

ON THE OTHER HAND, THE CONSPIRACY NUTS ARE SPOUTING SOME NONSENSE ABOUT A PLOT TO ELIMINATE CASH. THEY CLAIM THE INFORMATION CAME DIRECTLY FROM A SOURCE CLOSE TO THE PRESIDENT.

NOTHING LIKE A FEW *WELL-PLACED LEAKS* TO DEBUNK THE TRUTH.

ON A LESS CHEERY NOTE, WHILE YOU WERE BUSY TRYING NOT TO DIE, YOU, ME, AND TED WERE FIRED.

BUT, HEY-- BUREACRACY BEING WHAT IT IS-- MAYBE THEY WON'T GET AROUND TO CANCELING YOUR HEALTH INSURANCE UNTIL *AFTER* YOU'RE DIS- CHARGED FROM THE HOSPITAL.

NOW THAT MY GOOD NAME HAS BEEN RESTORED, I'M SURE I CAN FIND A WAY TO CHARGE THIS STAY TO THE HOUSE.

DR. REGAN?

THE NEW SHIFT IS HERE. I THOUGHT YOU MIGHT WANT TO GO OVER THE VACCINE PROTOCOL WITH THEM.

THANK YOU, GRACE. I'LL BE RIGHT THERE.

SO, WHAT WILL YOU DO?

START PREPARING FOR THE NEXT TIME.

OF COURSE, NOW THAT WE'VE LOST OUR ACCESS TO INSIDE INFORMATION, WE'LL BE LOOKING FOR NEW RECRUITS.

WE'LL NEED PEOPLE IN SENSITIVE GOVERNMENT POSITIONS. THE *HIGHER-RANKING,* THE BETTER.

YOU KNOW ANYONE WHO MIGHT BE INTERESTED?

AS MUCH FUN AS ALL OF THIS HAS BEEN, I THINK I'LL PASS.

SOME OF US STILL HAVE A JOB.

I WISH THIS MEETING COULD TAKE PLACE UNDER MORE PLEASANT CIRCUMSTANCES, ALBERT--

-- BUT I THINK IT'S SAFE TO SAY THAT SHIP HAS SAILED.

WHEN ANDERS SHOWED ME THE CONTENTS OF THIS ENVELOPE, I WAS SADDENED TO THINK THAT A MAN I'D TRUSTED TO DO RIGHT COULD ENGINEER SOMETHING SO UNSPEAKABLE.

WHAT IN *GOD'S NAME* DID YOU HOPE TO ACCOMPLISH?

TO FULFILL MY MANDATE.

YOUR MANDATE IS TO *PROTECT* THE AMERICAN PEOPLE FROM TERRORISM, NOT *UNLEASH IT UPON THEM.*

HOW SHOULD WE PROTECT THEM, THEN? PROFILING, ENHANCED INTERROGATION TECHNIQUES, MILITARY TRIBUNALS...

THOSE ARE COMMON-SENSE STRATEGIES, BUT IN AMERICA, COMMON SENSE WILL NEVER PREVAIL. THERE ARE FAR TOO MANY ACTIVISTS AND LAWYERS.

FROM BEHIND THAT DESK YOU TOLD ME THAT THE PEOPLE DEMAND *PERFECTION.* WELL, *FREEDOM* IS THE OBSTACLE THAT STANDS BETWEEN US AND THAT PERFECTION.

AND IF WE CAN'T *TAKE* FREEDOM, THEN WE MUST CONVINCE THE PEOPLE TO *GIVE IT AWAY.*

BY ANY MEANS NECESSARY?

WE ARE AT *WAR*, AND IN A TIME OF WAR IT IS *NECESSARY* TO SACRIFICE A FEW FOR THE SAFETY OF ALL.

YOU MAKE THE SAME DECISION EACH DAY THAT OUR SOLDIERS REMAIN IN COMBAT. THE ONLY DIFFERENCE IS THAT MY BATTLE PLAN WOULD HAVE *SUCCEEDED*.

DON'T *TEST ME*. I'D HAVE YOU TRIED FOR HIGH CRIMES, IF YOUR INDICTMENT WOULDN'T ALSO BE MY OWN.

I WILL, HOWEVER, ACCEPT YOUR *IMMEDIATE* RESIGNATION.

GOODBYE, THEN.

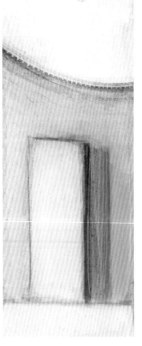

GOODBYE, ALBERT.

146

WE ARE OFFICIALLY UNEMPLOYED.

DO THEY INTEND TO PURSUE THE MATTER FURTHER?

NO.

AS I SUSPECTED, THE PRESIDENT'S DESIRE TO EXACT JUSTICE IS TEMPERED BY CONCERN FOR HIS *PUBLIC IMAGE.*

WHILE HIS MOTIVE WORKS IN OUR FAVOR, IT IS EXACTLY THE SORT OF FAILING THAT MAKES HIM SUCH A MEDIOCRE STATESMAN.

WHAT NOW?

NOW THE TASK OF KEEPING AMERICA SAFE WILL FALL TO MY REPLACEMENT, NO DOUBT AN INDIVIDUAL WITH A *POLITICIAN'S GIFT* FOR CAUTION AND SELF-PRESERVATION.

AS FOR *OUR* FUTURE--

-- THERE IS ALWAYS THE PRIVATE SECTOR.

BBBOOOOMMM!

AND NOW A BREAKING NEWS ALERT:

VIOLENCE ROCKED PENNSYLVANIA AVENUE MINUTES AGO, AS AN AUTOMOBILE EXPLOSION KILLED HOMELAND SECURITY SECRETARY ALBERT KEENE, HIS CHIEF OF STAFF, AND HIS DRIVER.

NOT MUCH IS KNOWN AT THIS TIME, BUT THE EXPLOSION APPEARS TO HAVE BEEN A TARGETED ATTACK.

ALREADY ONBOARD AIR FORCE ONE, THE PRESIDENT ISSUED THE FOLLOWING STATEMENT:

"ALBERT KEENE DEDICATED HIS LIFE TO THE SAFETY OF THIS GREAT NATION. IF HIS DEATH IS PROVED TO BE INTENTIONAL, THEN WE WILL FIND THOSE RESPONSIBLE--

"--AND THEY WILL BE BROUGHT TO JUSTICE."

END.